SHAMUS GOES WEST

by

Carolyn Gilman Middleton Guyer

Chapter One

Shamus O'Shaughnessy O'Rourke, left his family's farm in Ireland that had been devastated by the potato famine, and traveled by steerage to Ellis Island. The voyage was horrific with babies crying, vomit; nasty smells and bad food. He was allowed on deck for one hour a day. When the ship arrived in New York, he was relieved that he had survived.

He stood in line patiently for several hours, and finally was cleared to leave.

Shamus took a scrap of wrinkled paper from his pocket and showed it to the guard at the door. It was his cousin's address.

"Do you know how to get to this address?"

"Ask a policeman," he said in a nasty tone.

Shamus went outside, but he didn't see any coppers so he asked a lady.

She said, "Take a taxicab; they know all the addresses."

Shamus didn't have much money and he was afraid to use what he had. He walked and walked a long way. When he heard some music, he headed in that direction. A man with dirty clothes, a beard and a guitar played and sang off key. He had a cap on the ground and sometimes a pedestrian would drop in a few coins.

He stood near the man and listened for a while.

"Hey you," the man said. "Can you hold my place? I need to take a leak."

Shamus nodded. He didn't know what a leak was, but it didn't matter. He tuned the guitar and began strumming. He thought of home and closed his eyes and sang "Annie Laurie" in his beautiful baritone voice. Some people stopped to listen and a few put money in the hat. The man hadn't returned so he sang "Galway Bay" and more people dropped more money. He noticed the man had returned, but when he went to return the guitar, the man said, "Play some more."

He sang "Danny Boy" and a rousing "Who Put The Overalls in Mrs. Murphy's Chowder" and the money was filling the cap. It was growing dark. The man told him he had a wonderful voice and he could sing there any time. He took more than half the money out and gave it to Shamus. He doffed his cap, took his guitar and sauntered down the street.

Shamus continued to walk and ask people where the address was located.

Most people shook their heads or told him to ask someone else. He was outside a building with lots of young people exiting. He went and stood inside the door. He saw a door with a sign that said 'men's room' and he opened the door to see what kind of a room was for men. It was a loo and he was happy to see it. After he washed his hands and face, he came out, bumping into a young lady with red curly hair and a lovely smile.

"Sorry," he murmured.

"You look lost," she said.

He showed her the address and she said, "it's not far from where I am going."

She led to a bus stop and pointed
out the sign and the bench to him.
When the bus came, he handed the driver
a bill.

The driver growled, "no change."

His companion, Maureen O'Flaherty,
paid for him and he offered her the
bill. She gave him some coins back.

The bus stopped several times, but
it was a while before Maureen said it
was their stop.

They shared histories and laughed a
lot. Shamus thought it was nice to
laugh. Maureen was going to night
school to better herself and be able to
get a better job. She worked at a
diner serving people, but she didn't

like it much. She wanted to be a
nurse. Shamus thought that was a grand
idea.

"Do you think I can go to night
school?" he asked.

"Of course," Maureen said. "First,
you have to find your cousin, get a
job, get a place to live and save
money. Everything in America costs
money."

When they exited the bus, Maureen
said, "I go this way, but your address
is down that street and to the left.
The number will be on the outside of
the building and this number" pointing
to the paper, "is the apartment number.
It will be on the door of your

cousin's place."

Shamus walked down the broken sidewalk in front of rows of houses. He was still carrying his box that was tied with rope and held his worldly possessions. He soon caught on to the way the numbers were posted and found the building easily. The door was locked. He sat on the top step and dozed off until he heard the door behind him open. He jumped up, grabbing the door just before it closed. He climbed the stairs and then another set of stairs and then another before he found the apartment number. He knocked.

The door opened slightly and a man

peered out. It was not his cousin.

"I'm looking for my cousin,
McDougall O'Rourke." Shamus said.

The man opened the door wider.

"Your cousin used to live here, but
he moved to Boston. Come in and I will
get you his address. A fine man he is
and we shared many a pint in happier
times." He left the room and returned
with the address. Shamus copied it
down on the back side of his wrinkled
paper.

Shamus put his box down inside the
door and followed the man to a tiny
kitchen where a woman was cooking.

"This is Mick's cousin, from
Ireland," he told her. He got out a

bottle and two glasses and poured

drinks. Shamus would rather have had

the stew the woman was stirring, but

took the drink.

"How do I get to Boston?" he asked.

"Is it far?"

The man said, "my name is Farrin.

Yes, Boston is many miles away. You

will have to take a train from Grand

Central Station. Do you have a place

to stay? If not, you could sleep here.

We don't have an empty bed, but we can

give you a blanket to put on the

floor."

The woman dished out two bowls of

stew and gave one to each man. Two

small heads peered around the corner

and she told them to come and eat.

"This is my son Timothy and my son Frederick." Farrin said. We have two more and one on the way."

"Congratulations," said Shamus. He couldn't think of anything else. "I appreciate your hospitality."

Farrin poured another drink. "Want to go around to the pub and meet some of the guys?" he asked.

Shamus declined and took the blanket offered and laid down on the floor in the front room. He was asleep quickly.

When he woke up, the woman was leaving with the children and Farrin was no where in sight.

"Good morning," she said. "There's some tea on the stove and some biscuits in the oven. I'll be back as soon as I see the children off to school."

He smiled at her. She couldn't help but notice what a handsome man he was and she smiled back.

When she returned, Shamus had drank two cups of tea and eaten two biscuits which were surprisingly good. He thought there was cinnamon in them.

"How do I catch a bus to Grand Central Station?" he asked her.

She shrugged.

"There's a bus stop at the end of the street, but I don't know where it goes," she said. "I guess you could ask the driver."

He thanked her and when he shook hands, he gave her some bills.

"No need," she said and tried to give them back, but he wouldn't take them.

"I'll write and let you know when I get to Boston," he said.

He asked the bus driver how to get to Grand Central and the driver growled, "get on. Sit close and I'll tell you when to get off and you take bus thirty-two."

"What does that mean?" asked Shamus, holding out his hand with coins in it. The bus driver took two of the coins and dropped them in the slot.

"It's the number of the bus," he said angrily. He pointed to a number printed near the door. "This is fourteen. Now get on with you, you're holding up the line."

Shamus quickly sat down. He got off when the bus driver said, "change here for Grand Central."

The rest of the ride was uneventful and the bus pulled up in front of a large, impressive building, with a sign the read Grand Central Railway Depot."

CHAPTER TWO

     Shamus asked questions and found

out how to buy a ticket to Boston and

what track to take and settled down to

wait. He boarded and found a seat.

When the conductor came by and asked

for his ticket, Shamus asked if there

was food on the train. The conductor

ignored him. Shamus dozed. Someone

tapped him on the shoulder, he looked

up to see the conductor who motioned

him to move over.

     "My name is Alfred," the conductor

said. "Where are you from?"

"County Cork," Shamus answered shortly.

"I'm from Dublin many years ago. I bet this is very confusing to you, right?"

Shamus nodded.

"Where are you going?"

"South Boston," he answered, "I think."

"When you get off the train, go outside and look for bus number twenty-two and ask the driver to let you off at your street."

"Thanks," said Shamus. "Could you explain this money to me?"

The conductor took the bills from

him and educated him as to their denominations and how much they equaled in pounds and pence. Shamus caught on quickly.

The conductor looked at him sideways and said suspiciously, "You didn't steal this, did you?"

Shamus told him the story of singing and the man and his leak.

"By the way," said Shamus, "Why would a man leak?"

The conductor laughed uproariously and slapped his knee. When he explained, Shamus blushed and then laughed.   "It's a story to tell your grandchildren some day," the conductor said as he walked off laughing.

"By the way, the next car," he pointed, "is a dining car. Go there and sit down and someone will give you something to eat. You have to pay extra; it's not included in your ticket."

Shamus ate heartily and tipped the waiter.

Shamus found the right bus; showed the driver the name of the street and sat down close by. When the driver told him it was his stop, he got out; found the name of the street and looked for the number on the house.

CHAPTER THREE

Mary O'Rourke opened the door to see her handsome cousin-in-law, Shamus, standing there with a box tied with a rope and a glad, happy smile on his tired face.

She threw himself around his neck and cried, "Oh Shamus, I'm so happy to see you. How did you get here? How is everyone? Are you alone? Come in, come in."

She led him through the tiny apartment to a warm, cozy kitchen. There was a braided rug under the table and curtains at the window. There was a pot of tea brewing and good smells were coming from the oven.

"The O'Rourke will be so happy to see you," she told him. "He's at work and will come home at dinner time."

She poured him tea and warmed up two scones left over from breakfast. They talked and talked and Mary laughed at all his difficulties along the way. She told him the twins, Rodney and Rohan, were in school; Shannon and the baby were asleep and she was 'with child'. As if on cue, a baby began to cry and as soon as his nappie was changed, Mary brought him out to see his Uncle Shamus. He gladly held Padraig, nicknamed Paddy, and bounced him around. Mary took him away to feed him and Shannon peeked around the door.

"Hey," Shamus said softly, "I'm your Uncle Shamus."

She ran away.

When Rodney and Rohan came from school, they screamed, "Uncle Shamus, Uncle Shamus, how did you get here?"

"By ship and bus and train," he said laughingly, hugging the two look-a-likes. He bet they gave their teacher fits and bits, just as he and Mick did back in the day.

Mary scurried around the kitchen preparing dinner and Shamus kept the children occupied with stories and games and funny jokes. When the door opened, his cousin McDougall O'Rourke entered. He dropped his empty lunch sack and grabbed Shamus.

"How did you get here?" he yelled.
"Mary, Mary, did you see who's here? I
can't believe my sore eyes!"

Mary laughed. "Yes, O'Rourke I see
him."

They spent dinner time telling old
stories and new ones and when the
children were falling asleep, Shamus
helped carry them to bed. They all
slept in one room.

"We don't have a spare bed,"
McDougall said, but proudly added, "we
have a divan."

"It's better than the floor,"
Shamus said and they all laughed.

Once the children were down, the

O'Rourke brought out a whiskey bottle and poured two healthy drinks. He gave Mary a small glass of sherry.

"Let's make some plans."

Mary nodded.

"First, you need a job," the O'Rourke said. "I am a longshoreman on the docks and they are always hiring. The work is hard and the hours long, and the pay is low. You can go with me tomorrow and I'll show you the hiring office. How are your muscles?" He reached over and squeezed his cousin's upper arm. "Just as a thought," he continued, "weak as a kitten. You'll soon toughen up."

Shamus bragged, "I can still take

you down any time."

The cousins looked like brothers

and many had mistaken them for twins.

The O'Rourke said, "I doubt it."

He rolled up his sleeve, as did Shamus

and they did a bit of arm wrestling.

When Mick won most of the rounds,

Shamus said it was because he had

traveled so far. They all laughed.

Mary went to bed, but the men

stayed up til the wee hours, talking

about home and people they knew.

Finally, the bottle was empty; the men

were drowsy and they slept soundly.

When Shamus got to the hiring

office that Mick had pointed out, he

filled out a form and put Mick as his

reference. The man who interviewed him looked it over.

"You must be Mick's brother," he said smiling.

"I'm his cousin," Shamus replied.

"You're hired," the man said. "Frankie," he called out the door and a skinny, pale man showed up. "This is Mick's cousin, Shamus. Show him the ropes." He shook hands and Shamus followed Frankie.

The O'Rourke hadn't been kidding when he said the work was hard and the hours long. Shamus thought potato farming was tough, but it was nothing compared to loading and unloading ships; moving pallets around; and keeping up with more experienced longshoremen.

Shamus fell asleep while eating dinner.

CHAPTER FOUR

After three months, Shamus could keep up with the best of them; he and Mick made a fine team. The boss smiled at them and praised them whenever he checked the docks.

On Sundays, they went to Saint Cecelia's and Shamus prayed for all his relatives on the far shore and asked for forgiveness for any sins he may have committed.

One Sunday, he glanced up to see Maureen O'Flaherty, the aspiring nurse, who had helped him in New York.

"Well," she said, "it's a small world isn't it?"

They shook hands and she told him she had graduated and moved to South Boston with her sister.

"The jobs are better here."

Every Saturday, the men lined up for their pay which was handed to them in small envelopes. Mick and Shamus would stop at the postal station and put one-fourth of their pay on a money gram which they sent to Ireland. Shamus gave Mary onc-fourth when they got home. Sometimes they stopped at the pub, and Shamus or Mick would win more money in arm wrestling matches.

They seldom lost, but they never wrestled each other in public. Shamus put one-fourth of his earnings in an old sock he stored in the box he had brought from Ireland. He often bought the children candy or toys or clothes. Once he gave Mary a pretty set of dishes he found in the second-hand store.

One day he was called to the Office at work.

"i want you to meet, Mr. William Bandforth, the boss of Union 345," the hiring man said. "Mr. Bandforth, this is Shamus O'Rourke, one of your most out-standing workers."

They shook hands and exchanged some

pleasantries.

"Is there anything you would like changed?" Mr. Bandforth asked. He always asked this question, but the workers had answered that everything was good.

But not Shamus.

"Yes," he said. "I would like to see a Suggestion Box installed."

Mr. Bandforth looked surprised and then told the hiring man to put one up.

"Anything else?" he asked.

"Yes," said Shamus. "I would like to go to night school and learn how to be a newspaper man, but I don't know where to go or who to ask. Do you know?"

"Now, why would he tell you that?" blurted out the hiring man. "We would lose one of our most productive workers."

Mr. Bandforth held up his hand at this outburst.

"I will send some pamphlets around to you. Have a nice day."

True to his word, the pamphlets were delivered with his next pay envelope and Shamus poured over them. Mick shook his head at Shamus. Mary was more supportive.

Shamus asked for a day off and the hiring man grudgingly gave it to him with the admonishment that his pay would be docked.

Shamus went to the address on one of the pamphlets, but after asking numerous questions, he realized the classes commenced too early in the evening for him to attend. His disappointment was palpable. He went to his second choice and learned that they started their classes later and he could begin the next week; attending three nights. He paid the fees and bought second-hand books and went home a happy man.

Mick congratulated him, but he was disappointed that Shamus didn't want to continue to work with him.

"It will be a long time before I graduate," he assured Mick,"and even then, I will arm wrestle at the pub

with anyone you send my way." The two

men laughed,

CHAPTER SIX

     Every Sunday at mass, Shamus saw
Maureen, but she had a beau much to his
disappointment. They became fast
friends and she often gave him advise
on what classes he should take.

     Shamus was very intelligent and
learned everything they threw at him.
He was the professors' favorite. He
always had answers and he always had
his homework done. He was disappointed
when the school closed for the summer
vacation, but he signed up for fall and
looked forward to it.

When the fall came around, he was happy to be back in night school. He completed the courses and took more.

One day the hiring man senT for him. He went reluctantly and Mick looked at him sadly.

"I told you nothing good would come from trying to go above your station," Mick whispered.

When Shamus entered the office, Mr. Bandforth was with the hiring man and shook hands with Shamus. He inquired about school and what was Shamus studying and how were his grades. Shamus enjoyed the talk.

Mr. Bandforth cleared his throat.

"One of the suggestions put in the

box asks that the Union print a newsletter. I believe you could be the man for the job. It would entail learning how to operate a mimeograph machine and order supplies. You would have an office in this building and the use of the secretarial pool in order to type it out. I could speak to the night school and see if they would give you some credits. Of course this new position would entitle you to a raise as well."

Shamus was over joyed.

He shook hands with Mr. Bandforth. The hiring man was scowling, but Shamus felt he could win him over eventually.

Mick and Shamus went to the pub and

got drunk. Mary was angry with them.

She had been worried when they didn't

come home at the usual time and it

wasn't their "pub night". After she

heard why; she relented and was as glad

as Shamus.

"I'll miss you cousin," Mick said

sloppily and hugged Shamus.

Mary said, "it's not like he's

moving."

Shamus reported to the hiring man

who called Frankie to the door and told

him to initiate Shamus in his new

position. Shamus wore his best suit;

he had polished his shoes and got a

haircut.

The office he was given was so

small he could hardly turn around in it, but he didn't mind. He worked a mock-up of his first newsletter and asked the hiring man to approve it. The next day, it came back with some changes and Mr. Bandforth had written a piece to be included in it.

Shamus put a notice by the suggestion box asking for any information the workers would like to see in their newsletter; such as birthdays, anniversaries, new additions to their families; and promotions. He asked the men to put them under his door and he was overwhelmed with the amount of notices he got. He called this column "Our Families" and everyone read it first. The newsletter came out monthly and then bi-monthly as its popularity spread around the docks.

The night school had agreed to give him extra credit for his new position which helped him on his way to graduation.

Mr. Bandforth gave him a raise.

CHAPTER SEVEN

When Shamus graduated from night school with a degree in journalism, lots of people came to the ceremony; even Mr. Bandforth and his wife. Mick was puffed up like a bullfrog's throat. He told everyone several times over that this was his cousin.

It was early the next month when

the hiring man sent Frankie to fetch

Shamus; there was someone here to visit

him.

"I'm Jansen Fletcher," the

gentleman said, "editor of the

Gazette."

Shamus shook his hand and said, "I

think everyone in Boston knows who you

are, sir. What can I do for you?"

Mr Fletcher replied, "is there

somewhere we can talk in private?"

"Of course. Let's go to my

office."

Shamus was a little shy of showing

such an important man his little cubby

hole office, but he did.

"I am here, Mr. O'Rourke, to offer

you employment as a junior reporter on my paper. I have been following your Union Newsletter and I am greatly impressed by your fine writing."

Shamus was surprised.

"I would be honored," he said. "I have to give Mr. Bandforth a month's notice. He has been so very kind to me."

"Well," said Mr. Fletcher, "William Bandforth and I have been friends for more years that I care to mention. He was the person that pointed out to me what fine work you do. I don't think he will be surprised."

He told Shamus the hours and the pay and some of his duties.

"You will be following a seasoned
reporter around for a while until you
get the hang of it. I will expect you
to report to work in one month."

He stood and the men shook hands.

"You won't have a fancy office like
this," he joked. "Everyone works out
of one large news room."

Shamus laughed and thanked him. He
couldn't wait to get home to tell Mick
and Mary.

The month was going by slowly.
Frankie brought his replacement by and
Shamus trained him as best he could.
The young man was nervous and his
writing didn't meet the standards that
Shamus had for himself.

The Union boss, Mr. Bandforth, gave Shamus a big going away party on his last day. When Shamus was leaving, he put an envelope in his hand and wished him good luck.

Mick took Shamus to the pub where they drank until late and staggered home, holding on to each other, singing dirty Irish ditties. Shamus thought it had been a grand day.

"Did you know," Shamus told Mary at breakfast, "that the Leprechauns have hammers? They crawl into your ears when you drink too much and beat your brains."

Mary laughed.

Mick gave Mary a dirty look,

slapped Shamus on the shoulder and left
for work.

CHAPTER EIGHT

     Shamus and Mary went shopping.
They went to several stores before they
found the right suit and Shamus bought
three. They purchased shoes, socks,
and dress shirts with high collars,
like the one that Mr. Fletcher had been
wearing. They went to the stationers

and bought pens, pencils, notepads
(both small and large) and colored
pencils. Shamus bought coloring books
and crayons for the children.

They ate lunch at the counter in
the Five and Ten Cent Store. They were
so loaded down with packages, they
could hardly walk back.

They laughed and joked and had a
good time. It is so nice to have some
coin you can spend, thought Shamus.

Mary sent Shamus to the grocers
with a list. After collecting the baby
and Shannon from the lady next door,
she waited for the twins to come from
school. She made some tea and rubbed
her feet and relived the day in her

mind. When Shamus kicked the door, she opened it to find him loaded down with much more foodstuff than she had put on the list. He was followed by the grocers delivery boy who was also loaded down.

"Did you leave anything for other people to buy?" laughed Mary.

"I'm a growing boy," he smiled.

The weekend was pleasant and when they went to St. Cecilia's for mass, Shamus was congratulated on his good fortune. Father O'Malley blessed him.

Monday was windy and cool. Shamus donned his new clothes and after breakfast, took his brown bag lunch, his supplies and left for the bus. His stomach was fluttering. He had been so afraid of being late that he got to the downtown newspaper building thirty minutes early. He found a diner nearby and drank some tea and ate a muffin.

A doorman opened the door for him. He entered a huge rotunda. There was a long counter and three men were standing at intervals. He approached the first one.

"I am to report to work today at nine," he said.

The man said "Good morning Sir. Please sit on that bench," he pointed to the side "someone will come for you soon."

He had no sooner sat down when a

lady approached. She had a notebook in her hand and looking down at it, she said, "Mr. O'Rourke?"

Shamus nodded and she told him to follow her. She had on a very becoming suit with matching jewelry and shoes. Her hair was pinned up without a strand out of place. Shamus admired her.

She took him up marble stairs and to an office where she sat behind a big desk and motioned him to sit before her. She handed him paper after paper, which he read and signed each. Neither spoke.

"Follow me." She rose and exited a door to the rear of the office. There was an older lady behind a counter.

"This is Shamus O'Rourke," she told the lady and went out of the room.

"My name is Maggie," the lady said. "I will be taking pictures for the 'new hires wall' and for your identification tag. You must wear it at all times in this building and while on newspaper business. Your badge will be blue which means you are a reporter." She had on a yellow badge. Maggie took several pictures and then left to develop them. Two other people were brought in but no one spoke.

"This isn't a very friendly place," thought Shamus. "I hope the reporters are kinder."

When Maggie returned, she

instructed Shamus to pick out which pictures he wanted to be put on the 'new hire wall' and which to put on his badge. He must return the rest.

As if by some unheard communication, the first lady appeared.

"Come with me," she said and reached for the doorknob.

Shamus put his hand on top of hers and asked, "What is your name?"

She looked startled.

"You may call me Miss Veronica," she said frostily. She emphasized the 'miss'.

He let her hand go and she took him to the elevator. They boarded and went to floor three. It opened up to a huge room with many desks and people hurrying and scurrying around. Miss Veronica led him to the back of the room and showed him his desk. It was number forty. She ordered him to deposit his supplies in the desk and when he opened it, he discovered it was already filled with the same items he had purchased. He blushed and felt stupid. He put them in the bottom drawer along with his lunch.

"We have a dining room on the second floor," Miss Veronica informed him. "Most of us eat there as the prices are extremely low."

A young man with shirt sleeves rolled up by garters and a pencil behind his ear, rushed by and then turned back.

"Are you O'Rourke?" he asked. "Why of course your are – number forty. I am Frosty Shepherd, your trainer." He held out his hand and Shamus shook it.

"Shamus O'Rourke," he said, "your trainee."

"Thank you Miss Veronica," Shamus said.

"Come on O'Rourke," Frosty said. "I just got notice of a fire at the Bellevedere Hotel. We have to hurry." He rushed away and Shamus grabbed a note pad and pen. Shamus had a hard time keeping up with the frisky young man.

Frosty said, "Just follow my directions and watch what I do. It will be a while before you write."

Shamus enjoyed the hustle and bustle, both the rushing to disasters and the business of the newspaper room. Several reporters introduced themselves. Frosty told them Shamus was the latest new 'hot shot' found by Mr. Fletcher. They laughed.

One man said, "Irish, are you?" and turned away without shaking hands.

Frosty shrugged.

"If we want a lunch break, we had better take it now," said Frosty when there was a lull. He was typing at a high rate of speed and finishing, ripped out the page and left it on Shamus's desk.

"Read it when we get back."

They went to the elevator and took it down one floor. It opened to a huge dining room with many tables, covered with white tablecloths. There were flowers in vases on each table. The instant they sat down, uniformed waiters placed water glasses, tea cups, a pot of tea and a carafe of iced water.

"My usual," said Frosty. "This is Shamus, number forty."

The waiter nodded and waited for his order.

There was no menu and Shamus asked

for soup and sandwich, deciding that would be safest. The waiter frowned and left.

Frosty talked to almost everyone who came or left and most of it was gibberish to Shamus. He was upset.

The rest of the day was rush here, rush there, read Frosty's writings and then rush somewhere else. Sometimes they took a photographer with them and sometimes not. Shamus got up the nerve to point out a few grammatical errors and Frosty changed them with a red pencil. The rest of the week was the same and Shamus was tired and discouraged when Friday arrived.

"You can leave now," said Frosty.

"I have some place to be."

He rose and put on his suit coat, locked his desk and straightened the papers on top. Mr. Fletcher appeared.

"How is everything Shamus?" he asked.

Suddenly the entire room was quiet and everyone stared. Mr. Fletcher didn't often come out of his office – he sent for someone when he wished to speak to them.

"It's all a little confusing," Shamus blurted out. He blushed.

"Frosty," said Mr. Fletcher sternly. "It is your duty to see that Shamus is not confused and he understands, not only what we do here, but the reasons behind it."

Frosty threw Shamus a dirty look and said, "Yes sir."

"Did you get lunch?" Mr. Fletcher asked solicitously.

Shamus nodded.

Mr. Fletcher smiled at him. "It will get easier, but if you want to ask questions, just knock on my office door." He pointed to the back of the room where a frosted window on the door read 'Editor'.

Frosty's mouth dropped open. He turned away before Mr. Fletcher could see how startled he was.

The Editor picked up the paper from Shamus's desk.

"Is this your work?" he asked.

"I was just helping Frosty with spelling."

Mr. Fletcher turned on Frosty.

"How long have your worked here?" he said angrily.

"Two years," he stammered.

"And you didn't have the nerve to come to me and ask to take a spelling class? What's wrong with you?" Mr. Fletcher was angry. "You clean out your desk; you're fired.

Shamus spoke up. "Wait, Mr. Fletcher, you can't do that. He is my trainer and we work well together. He is a good reporter. We will make a good team."

Mr. Fletcher looked startled at this outburst.

"Get back to work," he said to Frosty loudly. He turned to Shamus. "Take this paper home. You will write this column the way it should be written and bring it to my office tomorrow morning." He stalked off.

When Mr. Fletcher departed, Frosty hissed at him, "Why didn't you tell me you are some kind of big shot?" He stormed away.

CHAPTER NINE

Shamus went home, working over in his mind the day. Maybe he wasn't cut out for this work.

Shamus arrived at work a few minutes early and was waiting outside Mr. Fletcher's private office. Many of the reporters glanced at him; some glared at him. Frosty nodded to him. Mr. Fletcher's secretary arrived and unlocked the door. He looked sideways at Shamus, and mumbled good morning.

Mr. Fletcher arrived; hung up his suit coat; smoothed his hair and said, "Come with me, Shamus."

They got on the elevator together and went to the dining hall. The waiter hurried forward with coffee and pastries and set it on the table.

"Tea and water," Mr. Fletcher ordered.

He reached for the newly written article that Shamus had worked on far into the night. He read it carefully once, then twice. Shamus drank some tea and ate a pastry. It wasn't as good as Mary made.

"That is much better," he said. "I won't fire Frosty at your request, but

I am giving you a new trainer." He raised his hand and a man stepped forward.

"This is Johnson Jonas; meet Shamus O'Rourke, my protegee." Shamus stood and shook hands, looking Johnson in the eye. Everyone in the city knew Johnson Jonas; he was a prize-winning, star reporter.

Johnson sat down and helped himself to pastry. He nibbled at it and said, "You need a new pastry chef, Fletch. I've tasted much better."

"I agree," said Shamus. "My cousin Mary cooks delicious pastry; in fact, I'm getting fat."

"Does she want a job?" asked Mr.

Fletcher.

"No," Shamus said laughing.

Johnson said, "May I read his
article?"

Fletch handed it over.

Johnson read it quickly. "Not bad,
not bad at all."

Shamus felt he had passed some sort
of test.

Mr. Fletcher said, "Are you two
going to loaf around here all day or
are you going to work for your pay?"

Both Shamus and Johnson nodded and
laughed.

The day passed quickly and Johnson
explained everything they did; why they
did it; and how to write it up for

print. Shamus was a fast learner and asked good questions. Johnson reported to Fletch on the quiet that Shamus was going to be a great reporter.

CHAPTER TEN

The time flew by with Johnson as his trainer. They made a great team and worked side by side. Soon it was winter and Shamus took an afternoon off to buy boots and a heavy coat and warmer shirts. He took Mary with him and they had a grand time.

By the time spring melted the snow and trees budded, Shamus was a full-fledged reporter. Most of the other employees ignored him or merely nodded and, except for Johnson, he had no friends. He missed the camaraderie he had shared with Mick and went to the pub with him whenever he could but it wasn't quite the same.

One night in late summer, he came home to find Mary and Mick and several neighbors having a party in his honor for having worked as a reporter for one whole year. They drank and sang and played parlor games. The food was delicious. Shamus felt happier than he had in a long time.

It was several days later, when Mr. Fletcher sent Miss Veronica to Shamus's desk with a message to see him at five o'clock. He asked Johnson if he knew what it was about, but he only shrugged.

At five o'clock (always one for punctuality) Shamus knocked on Mr. Fletcher's door. His secretary answered and told him to go in Mr. Fletcher's office and wait. He left.

"Sorry, I'm late," Mr. Fletcher said, hurrying in. "Will Bandforth and I were at a meeting together. There is probably going to be a strike of longshoremen; they want better pay."

He shuffled some papers on his desk.

"Have you traveled much?" he asked Shamus.

Shamus shook his head. He was

mulling over what a strike might do to Mick and his family.

"I have this request from the Board of Directors to send someone out west to write articles regarding a huge gold strike going on at Sutter's Mill. Someone claims they found the largest nugget ever. Do you know much about it?"

"Only what I read in the papers," Shamus said laughing. Fletcher laughed also.

"Well, I want you to pack your bags and leave next Monday on the train."

The door opened and Miss Veronica entered. She smiled at Shamus.

"Here is your schedule and train

tickets," she said. "You have to change in New York and again in Chicago. Here is money for hotels, stagecoaches, and meals." She handed him two banded sums of money and a voucher for him to sign. She gave him a telegraph address to be used to file his reports and make any requests.

"Try not to get scalped by Indians," she said and left.

Mr. Fletcher stood up. "I second that," he said laughing. "Don't be afraid to request anything you need. I expect at least one article a week and more if you can handle it. This is exciting news and everyone will be expecting a lot from you. There are members of the Board who are anxious to invest in gold if this story is true."

"Thank you, Mr. Fletcher," Shamus said and shook his hand. "How long am I to stay in the west?"

"As long as it take," was the answer. "See you when you report back."

Mick and Mary were happy and sad at the same time; as was Shamus.

"Will you see Indians?" asked Rohan.

"I bet there are train robbers." said Rodney.

"I'll let you know."

Shamus waited until the children were in bed and then told Mick and Mary about the Union strike that might come.

"Do you have enough to tidy you over for a while?" Shamus asked.

"I think so," said Mick. "We saved a lot of what you have been giving us."

Shamus wrote down where he would be and told them if there was an emergency to telegraph him. He would send a telegram when he knew where he was staying.

CHAPTER ELEVEN

Shamus boarded the train and took a window seat. He tried to speak to the conductor, but he was grouchy and walked away. When he got to New York, he got off and changed trains and when he got to Chicago, he changed again. The food was okay and the scenery was nice. It was sooty and dirty. He dozed now and again and in the evening, the conductor unfolded the seat into a bed. He had several books in his pack and he read them.

He had three hours in Chicago before his next train left, so he walked around the city. Like most cities, it was smelly and dirty and crowded with people of all kinds. He bought some peppermints and newspapers and magazines.   Once he was back on the train, he read and dozed and watched the scenery go by. It grew warmer and the soot bothered him more. He saw desert scenes and cacti and pale green bushes. "I am finally getting to the west," he thought.

After Denver he headed for Santa Fe, where he would have to rent a horse and buckboard or take a stagecoach. He was gazing out the window when he saw men in cowboy garb racing along side

the train. They had bandannas over

their mouths and their hats were pulled

low.

"Help, help," he yelled. "The

train is being robbed. The train is

being robbed."

He stood and pulled the emergency

cord that signified trouble and the

wheels screeched as the brakes were

applied.

The conductor came rushing through

the car.

"Who pulled the emergency?" he

yelled. "Who pulled the emergency

switch?"

"I did," said Shamus, "the train is

being robbed." He pointed out the window to the wranglers, now stopped and staring at the train.

"Are you crazy?" screamed the conductor. "Those cowboys always race the train. It's just a fun thing for them to do." He walked away muttering about 'crazy Irish' and stormed off the car. The engineer and his fire man met with him and Shamus saw them cursing and yelling at each other. Shamus was embarrassed.

The three men boarded the car and surrounded Shamus. They rough-handed him down the aisle and out of the car. They threw him down the steps onto the ground. The baggage car opened, and the handler threw his trunk off the train, almost hitting one of the cowboys.

It wasn't long before the train puffed away. Several faces were staring out the windows at him and he wished he could hide.

"What did you do?" asked one of the wranglers.

Shamus repeated his shameful story and the cowboys laughed at him.

"Slim, get Mellie," one cowboy, who appeared to be in charge, said. "The rest of you get back to work."

"Name is Pete," he said, shaking hands with Shamus, who told him his name.

"I ramrod for the BarMM," he said.

"What does that mean?" asked Shamus.

"I'm the boss," he said smiling.

Shamus nodded. They waited and Shamus wished he knew why they were waiting. He went to his trunk and righted it, discovering that one of the hinges had broken.

A buckboard pulled up, pulled by two large horses, and driven by a slim girl in the same cowboy outfit that Pete wore. Shamus couldn't remember ever seeing a gal in pants.

"Got thrown off?" she asked Shamus.

"I thought your men were outlaws," he said blushing.

She thought this was hilarious.

"Pete," she said, "I'll take this from here. Get those cows rounded up."

Pete tipped his hat, backed his horse up and took off.

"My name is Mellie Mims," she said, holding out her hand. Shamus shook it.

"I'm Shamus O'Rourke, reporter for the Gazette. I'm headed for the gold fields."

"You ain't going to strike it rich," Mellie said.

"I write articles for the newspaper, not dig for gold."

"Pan," she said, "it's known as panning for gold."

Shamus nodded.

"My ranch is the closest place, so
I might as well haul you over there.
Sooner or later someone will get you
into town and you can take another
train. This your stuff?" She pointed
to the broken trunk.

When Shamus nodded, she picked it
up and slung it into the back of the
buckboard. Shamus looked surprised;
both at her muscles and her lack of
letting a man do it for her.

"Get on," she said.

She climbed on the driver's seat
and Shamus sat beside her. The horses
were fast and she drove recklessly,
stirring up dust. It wasn't long
before she pulled up in front of a

large farmhouse. A man was sitting in a wheelchair on the porch.

"What's the matter?" he asked Mellie.

She jerked her thumb at Shamus and said, "City slicker got dumped off the train. Keep him until I get back." She rode off.

Shamus stood there looking at the man and wondering what to do.

"Name's Bradford Mims," he said finally.

"Shamus O'Rourke," he said.

"Irish, hey? Where you from?"

"Boston," Shamus answered.

A dark-skinned woman wearing a long calico dress and wiping her hands on an apron, came from the house.

"Hola," she said.

"What does that mean?" asked
Shamus.

"Hello in Spanish," answered
Bradford.

"Would you like food and drink?"
she asked.

"Of course he would, you idiot,"
yelled Bradford. "Get him cleaned up
and fed."

The woman dropped her eyes and
motioned Shamus to follow.

"Where are your things?" she asked
him as she showed him a brightly-lit
room decorated with striped rugs on the
wall and a narrow bed.

"In the back of Mellie's buckboard." Shamus answered.

He washed his face and hands in the bowl on the washstand and wiped them on a towel cloth. He took his suit coat off, rolled up his sleeves and smiled shyly at her.

"What's your name?" he asked.

"Maria, come with me," and she led him to a kitchen, motioned him to sit at the table and brought him strong, hot coffee, meat and seasonings wrapped in a tortilla and beans on the side.

Shamus ate it all and drank the coffee, even though he preferred tea.

"What is this called?" he asked.
Maria looked surprised.

"Don't you know what tortillas are?" she asked.

He shook his head.

"Go sit on the porch with the old man. The men will return in a while. Don't walk around or get into trouble."

Shamus nodded and did as he was told.

He was nodding off in the warm sunshine, when the wranglers returned, led by Mellie driving her buckboard. Pete grinned at him and took his steamer truck from the rear and walked into the house with it. Shamus assumed that Maria told him where to put it.

Mellie got down from her perch, handed the reins to a cowhand who led the buckboard away, and came onto the porch. She nodded to Shamus and kissed the old man on his forehead.

"How're you feeling, Pa?" she asked.

"How do you expect me to feel, stuck in this contraption?" he replied grouchily.

She went into the house.

When it was almost dark, Mellie came out and said, "Come on Shamus." She walked towards the bunkhouse. A fire was burning and there was a large pot hanging over it. The cowhands were standing around, each with a plate, spoon and wooden cup. A pot of coffee sat on the rocks at the edge of the fire.

Mellie handed Shamus a plate, spoon and cup.

"This is Cookie," she said. The man was holding a large ladle, and he nodded.

"Men," said Mellie, in a loud voice. "This is Shamus O'Rourke who got kicked off the train for thinking you guys were robbers." Everyone laughed and Shamus blushed. "He's a city slicker from Boston and he writes for a newspaper. If you are interested in seeing your name in print, tell him your story." She grinned at Shamus.

She raised her hands above her head and the men took off their hats and bowed their heads. She said a short prayer of thanks and Cookie began to ladle out the food. Maria came from the house and filled two plates with food and took them towards the house. Shamus figured they were for Bradford and herself.

After Shamus had his plate filled, he went and sat on a rock. Mellie sat down beside him. He learned that her father, Bradford, had been thrown from a wild bronco and busted his back more than five years ago.

"I run the ranch," she said sternly.

Mellie told him the size of the ranch, how many cows they owned, and

the number of cowboys she bossed
around.

Shamus asked her some questions and
she answered them. She appeared to
like his observations and figures.

One of the cowboys started to strum
a guitar (it was out of tune)and
another blew a mouth organ.

"Do you play?" the guitar-strumming
cowboy asked when he saw Shamus
watching him.

Shamus took the guitar from him and
tuned it up. He sang "In The
Gloaming," and "Sweet Betsy from Pike."
His handsome baritone soared through
the air and everyone clapped when he
was done.

A cowhand asked him if he knew a song and Shamus said, "if you sing it, I can play it." It was later than usual when they retired. The men had spoken kindly to him and as he and Mellie walked back to the house, she said, "You have a nice voice."

CHAPTER TWELVE

Shamus wasn't sure how long he would be stuck out here so he spent his days asking questions and learning as much as he could about ranch life. He picked up some interesting stories from the men and when he retired, took out a notebook and wrote many a tale; freely ignoring the truth.

Mellie knocked on his door one

evening, and when he opened it she said curtly, "I'll be going to town tomorrow at daybreak. Get your things packed if you want to go."

In some ways, Shamus was sorry to leave the ranch. He wondered how Mick and Mary would like living out here. He was sure the children would love it; life was certainly different here.

Mellie stopped at the train depot. Shamus offered her money as he thanked her and she shook her head and refused to take it.

"Maybe I'll see you around some time," she said.

Shamus bought a ticket and boarded for Santa Fe. He was nervous that he might get the same conductor, but he didn't. When he got to Santa Fe, he went to a hotel, rented a room, and slept like a log until the next day.

After partaking of breakfast he walked around the town. When he saw the telegraph office, he entered and asked if there was any telegrams for him. He had two. He sat outside on a bench and read them. One was from Mr. Fletcher wishing him a good journey and asking if he had any news. The other was from Miss Veronica informing him that the Bank of Santa Fe had a bank draft for him.

He went inside and sent Mick a telegram that said he arrived in Santa

Fe and all was well.

He went to the bank and showing his badge, received money from the teller.

The room he had rented was hot, stuffy and smelled like dirty socks. He went to 'Ma's Eats', ordered a pot of tea and some pastries. The waitress said they didn't have tea, but she would bring him coffee. He wrote two stories, one humorous one about the 'train robbery' and the other about ranch life. When they had been corrected to his liking, he went to the telegraph office and giving the man the special key that belonged to Mr. Fletcher, sent them off.

In the evening, he went to the

saloon near his hotel, but the men seemed tough and rough so he sought out another. This one was only slightly more refined. He had two whiskeys and left.

After talking to the stagecoach manager, he learned that he could take a stage the next day straight to the gold fields. The manager also informed him that if he wished to buy a horse or a horse and buggy, he could travel today and arrive sooner, but he declined. The stagecoach ran once a week to the fields.

Shamus went to the saloon and spent time talking to those men who looked as though they were miners. He asked

questions and bought drinks and felt
better informed about the gold fields.

CHAPTER THIRTEEN

     When Shamus arrived at the gold
fields he was surprised to see the
hundreds of men working for a chance to
become wealthy. There were large tents
set up with hand-written signs
advertising their businesses. There

were four 'ladies of the evening'
establishments and the 'ladies' called
to him as he walked by. He saw a sign
that read 'tents for rent' and rented
one so he would have a place to sleep.
It was roomy and set up on a wooden
platform. There was a cot and
blankets; a rickety table with a water
jug; and some pegs on the center post
where he could hang his clothes. He
counted six eating places; two supply
stores; and a land office. There were
ten saloons. He had to stay at least a
week because the stagecoach wouldn't be
returning until then. He had a feeling
he would be staying more than that.

     In the evening, Shamus entered the

"Gold Mine Saloon", the largest and best looking of them all. There were men playing cards, a piano player, a long wooden bar and a naked lady painted on a mirror hanging on the wall behind it. Shamus ordered a whiskey and wandered over to the piano.

"If you sing, go to it," the player said.

Shamus sang "O'er the Hills of Killarney" and several men cat-called and whistled when he finished. He sang a few more.

A large man with large hands came over to him and smiled.

"Do you arm wrestle?" he said.

"Don't do it," said the player.

"He's the champ 'round here."

Shamus said, "Well, I can give it a shot."

They cleared off a table and most of the men gathered around.

"The first one is free," the big man said. "They call me Champ."

"Shamus O'Rourke." He took out a bill. "I think we should get right to it – nothing for free."

Champ roared.

They were evenly matched, but Shamus put him down in the end.

"My arm slipped," Champ whined. He took out another bill.

Having observed his mannerisms, Shamus flipped him down quickly. The men muttered and murmured among themselves.

"Anyone else?" asked Shamus, rising. He bought a bottle of whiskey for Champ, shook hands and left. He slept restlessly, surrounded by guns going off, men yelling and whistling, horses galloping by and a woman screamed.

CHAPTER FOURTEEN

When the sun rose, so did Shamus.

"I've been looking for you," said Champ. "Where's your equipment?"

"Oh," said Shamus, "I'm a newspaper man here to write stories, not to pan for gold."

"Come with me to my claim," said Champ. His eyes were blood shot and his clothes were wrinkled and dirty.

Shamus wondered if he had a place to
stay.

"Want some coffee first? I'll
treat." said Shamus. Champ led the way
to one of the eaterys and a large woman
slammed down a pot of coffee, eggs,
toast and muffins. Champ showed him
where to get the plates and they helped
themselves, both eating heartily.

"I heard you singing," Champ said.
"Sounded good."

Shamus nodded.

"You are a good arm wrestler,"
Shamus said. "My cousin Mick showed me
a trick of the trade and I seldom lose.
You held your own well."

Champ smiled ruefully. "Didn't win

though."

They walked to Champ's diggings.
The plots were divided by stakes, each
with a number. Champ's was number ten.

"Been here long?" asked Shamus.

"About a year," Champ said. "Just
about ready to hang it up. At first, I
found some nuggets, but I think they
are all gone now; too many people."

While Champ worked, Shamus walked
around. Many of the men had seen him
the night before and greeted him;
others simply ignored him. It was a
long day; Shamus sat at the site side
and wrote down his observations.

Champ and Shamus ate dinner at a
different diner and then walked to the

saloon. Shamus sang a few songs with the piano man. Several men offered to arm wrestle him but he said he would another time. He showed Champ where he stayed.

"How about you?" he asked Champ. "Do you have a tent?"

Champ looked down and scuffed the ground. "Naw, I gave it up; just bed down on my site."

Shamus went to the man who had rented him his tent and paid for another one close by.

"Ah, shucks," said Champ. "You didn't have to do that."

"My newspaper pays for it," Shamus lied.

Champ and Shamus were friends and the men seldom saw one without the other. One night Champ won some money arm wrestling and left without Shamus. Although Shamus wondered where he went, he didn't ask. One good thing about their friendship was they knew when to give the other one privacy.

"Tomorrow," Shamus told Champ, "I am traveling by stagecoach to Santa Fe. I have to send my articles to my boss. Would you like to come with me? I'll be gone a week."

Champ frowned, "I can't leave my plot that long. I'd be cleaned out by the time I returned. Why don't you just rent a horse and come back?"

Shamus blushed. "The truth is, I don't know how to ride."

Champ laughed. "We could get a buggy and be gone one day."

Champ hired a 'sitter' for his diggings; a young man who made money watching sites.

The stagecoach ride was bumpy and dusty and they were thirsty when they arrived in Santa Fe. Shamus went to the telegraph office and picked up several telegrams. He sent three stories to Mr. Fletcher, as well as telling him that he hadn't located a 'large nugget' yet. He sent a telegram to Mick and Mary telling them he was fine.

Champ was busy locating a buggy and a horse that he could rent, but not one was available. When he met up with Shamus, he said, "No one wants to rent."

"How about buying?" asked Shamus.

The two men went to the bank and Shamus withdrew money to purchase the animal and cart. The stableman was happy to sell them a workhorse and a farm wagon. They haggled over the price.

Shamus and Champ went to the hotel. They collected the trunk and belongings that Shamus had left there and he checked out. He gave the clerk a fair tip. Champ put the trunk in the farm

wagon and before they went to the
saloon. they visited the feed store and
stocked up on grain for the horse.
They went to the grocers and bought a
few supplies; Shamus stopped at the
newspaper and bought the latest
edition; and then entered the saloon.
Shamus sang and received praise. Champ
won many arm wrestling bouts and had
collected a fair sum of money.

They camped out under the stars
outside of the town and left early next
morning. Champ taught him how to
harness the horse and hitch the buggy.
They were soon on their way and the
weather was lovely with just a hint of
a breeze.

Champ continued to work his claim
without much luck anc Shamus continued
to interview and write his stories.

CHAPTER FIFTEEN
The next time Shamus went to the

city, he took the stagecoach and told
Champ he would be back in a week. He
had a lot of work to do and needed to
have some time alone. He rented a room
at the hotel and collected his
telegrams and latest newspapers. He
wrote some articles and shipped them
off to Boston. He wrote a long letter
to Mick and Mary and enclosed money.
He told them that he wished they could
all move to the west and maybe they
should talk about it. He didn't know
when he would be home. He missed them
all.

Mr. Fletcher sent him a telegram
that his articles were clever and
popular, but he wanted Shamus to find

the nugget, if there was one.

Shamus sent back a terse telegram: I'm looking.

After his errands were complete, he went back to the hotel to rest and read until dinner time. The clerk waved to him and gave him a piece of paper. It read: I'm in Room 2. It was signed Mellie Mims.

Shamus knocked on Room 2 and Mellie opened the door. She smiled at him. Mellie was wearing a calico dress and slippers. Her hair was hanging loosely down her back and she look stunning. Shamus smiled and felt his heart thump.

"What are you doing here?" Shamus asked.

"Once or twice a year I come to the city to order various things and supplies and feel like a woman for a few days. May I take you to dinner?"

"Let me go to my room and change," Shamus said.

When they were settled at the table, they ordered wine and a full meal. They talked and laughed and took turns sharing antidotes from the past. The waiter came to their table and cleared his throat. When Shamus looked up, the waiter said, "Sir, we are past closing time."

"Oh," laughed Shamus, "We got carried away." He added a hefty tip to the bill which pacified the disgruntled waiter.

Mellie and Shamus sat in the rocking chairs on the hotel porch and enjoyed the full moon and the brilliant stars. Shamus and Mellie regretfully parted but agreed to meet for breakfast. Shamus kissed Mellie on the check at her door.

Breakfast was enjoyable until Mellie announced that her return ticket was scheduled for the afternoon.

"I wish you would come back with me," Mellie said wistfully. "Maybe when your assignment is complete, you will spend a few days at the ranch."

"I would like that," Shamus said shyly.

Shamus purchased some new clothes and a cowboy hat and bandannas. He packed his derby away and threw out his old clothes.

CHAPTER SIXTEEN

When the day came for the stagecoach to travel to the gold fields, Shamus was more than ready to go. Next time he would drive the wagon so he could return at his choice.

After settling into his tent, saying hello to several people he knew, he went looking for Champ. The site was being worked by a stranger who told Shamus he had bought Champ out. He didn't know where Champ was.

Shamus felt sad and when he went to the saloon later that evening, he took on all arm wrestling takers and beat them quickly. He drank a lot and staggered home.

The next morning, Shamus drank three cups of coffee and felt sorry for his head. He hardly touched his breakfast. A miner approached him; he was small and bent and shaggy.

"Are you Shamus?" he asked.

Shamus nodded and then wished he hadn't, because it made his head hurt even more, if possible.

"My name is Dinger," he said. "I wanted to talk some business with you." He kept turning left, then right and nervously checking out the other patrons. "Can we go somewhere else?"

Shamus nodded and they went to his tent.

Dinger checked around and then sat

on the ground. He whispered, "I have found the mother lode. I need to go to Santa Fe to check out how pure the gold is and check the land filing to see that it is fully covered, but I don't trust anyone to oversee my plot. You are one of the few people who ain't interested in finding gold and I think I can trust you. Also, even though everyone calls me Dinger, my true name is O'Flaherty.

Shamus said, "I could do that. Do you wish to drive my horse and buggy or take the stagecoach?"

"Well, I could get there and back quicker by buggy."

Dinger checked outside and around

the tent to see if anyone heard or saw
them.

"Meet me outside of town," he
whispered and crept away.

Dinger was ambling along slowly and
headed for the end of the plots.
Shamus kept him in sight as he talked
to various miners and asked about
Champ. When Shamus ran out of working
claims, he climbed a small hill and
watched Dinger enter a rocky area and
disappear. Shamus sat for a while and
then walked slowly to the place where
Dinger had last been seen.

"Psst; psst;" whispered Dinger from
the shadows; Shamus had passed by him.
Dinger led Shamus to a narrow

opening between very tall rocks and shuffled along. It was getting lighter and Shamus looked up to see a hole at the top of the cave that was letting in some light. Dinger circled a rock and stopped and pointed ahead. Shamus almost fell over and he felt very light headed. There, in front of the two men, was a gold wall, extending from floor to ceiling.

"Is that real gold?" Shamus asked when he could catch his breath.

"That's why I need to go to the city and have it checked." Dinger told him. "I can take it to the land office here, but then everyone would know and there are some really nasty people around. I have to keep this a secret until I get my mining operations in gear."

Shamus nodded.

"I can watch it for you," he said.

Dinger left with the cart and buggy. "I wonder if I will ever see it again," Shamus thought. "I'm not sure I trust Dinger; there is something odd here."

Shamus examined the cave, walking down one corridor and then another. He dropped a string behind him as he went so he could follow it back and not get lost. He found another wall of gold; not as big or as tall, but just as pretty. He climbed the outside of the cave and found the hole that let in the light. He could see the entire mining fields and town from the top and stayed there most of the day, writing and rewriting his stories.

Dinger returned, grinning like a baboon. He whispered to Shamus, "It's almost pure. A surveyor will be here in a week and then mining equipment will be delivered and I can start making money." He clapped his hands over his mouth.
"The most difficult thing is keeping it a secret."

Shamus nodded and went back to walking around, talking to miners and listening to their stories. He missed

Champ. He wrote a letter to Mellie and
another to Mick. He read the papers
front to back again in case he had
missed anything the first time.

CHAPTER SEVENTEEN

    Shamus was tired of the settlement
and decided to explore the desert. He
hitched the horse to the wagon; filled
a canteen with water and went for a
ride. He walked the horse and admired
the scenery. He wished Mellie was with
him; he really liked her and enjoyed
her company.

    He was day-dreaming when he was
surrounded by Indians. Their faces had

strange designs painted on them; they carried spears decorated with feathers, small stones and hair. Shamus hoped it wasn't from human scalps. Shamus felt his heart skip a beat, but he stopped his horse. He said hello pleasantly. An Indian came forward and pointed his finger.

"Shamus"?" he grunted.

Shamus nodded and said, "I'm Shamus."

He made hand gestures to a brave; he rode forward and climbed onto the wagon, sitting beside Shamus. He picked up the reins and slapped the horse, who moved forward. The Indian smelled strongly and Shamus learned that the braves rubbed bear fat on

themselves to ward off mosquitoes,

ticks and flies. Shamus sat still.

CHAPTER EIGHTEEN

     After a long time, the wagon,

surrounded by the braves, arrived at an

Indian encampment. The teepees were

tall and poles criss crossed out of the

hole at the top. The buffalo hides

that covered the sticks were decorated

with squiggles and circles and crosses.

Shamus wondered if they could be read

or were they just decorations. No one

had spoke to him all the way across the

desert.

     "I don't think they intend to hurt

me," Shamus thought.

When they stopped at a teepee with black smoke pouring out the top, the Indians dismounted and led the horses away. His driver unhitched the horse and led him away. When he returned, he motioned Shamus to come with him. They entered the smokey, smelly tent. It took a few minutes for Shamus to adjust his eyesight to the semi- darkness. An Indian saw cross-legged on the ground, muttering a chant over and over. He held a woven bowl with burning liquid and he waved the smoke with a long feather. On a low platform covered with blankets and buffalo robes lay a man; a white man. His eyes were closed.

Shamus walked over to the man and knelt by his side, exclaiming "Champ, Champ, is that you? Are you alive? Oh, Champ, I am so glad to see you. Speak to me, Champ."

The man opened his eyes and turned his head towards Shamus. He grinned.

"Hello Shamus," he said as tears came to his eyes. "I thought I would never see you again." He struggled to sit up and Shamus helped him. There were leaves stuck to him in at least two places.

"Are you hurt, old friend?" asked Shamus.

"Shot," he said. "Indians brought me here - made me better."

His voice was fading as he spoke and Shamus said, "Don't talk, Champ. Get all the rest you can."

The chanting continued and Shamus laid Champ down and covered him. He slept.

Champ went outside and asked, "Does anyone speak English?"

"Trappers," said the Indian that had first called him by name. "Two more moons."

Shamus nodded.

The Indian made motions of eating and drinking and Shamus nodded. He was led to a circle of rocks; inside was a fire burning low; bowls were on some of the rocks and a wooden trough was over

the fire and filled with some food;
some kind of stew. Shamus picked up a
bowl and dipped it into the liquid and
drank it. It was very bitter and
Shamus hoped that it wouldn't poison
him.

The Indian was watching him and
nodded. He took Shamus to a small tent
and pulled back the flap. It was
empty. There was a robe on the ground.
Shamus took off his coat and hat and
set them next to the robe. Again, the
Indian nodded. Shamus saw a shallow
pool and went there. He knelt down and
drank some water; wetting his face and
back of his neck and then his hands.
He earned another nod.

Shamus returned to the tent where Champ lay wounded and sat outside watching the Indians. Some of the children were playing a kicking game with a stone. Several of the women were weaving baskets and their fingers flew quickly making lovely designs. Shamus smiled at them and nodded. Two young girls came from the desert carrying baskets of berries and two bucks returned carrying the carcass of an animal between them on a pole resting on their shoulders.

Shamus wondered where the braves that had brought him here, had gone. He wished he could ask questions about how they lived. He vowed to remember as much as he could so he could write a

story about them for the newspaper.

CHAPTER NINETEEN

     The Indians began to stir and move
around. They went to the communal fire
and filled their bowls and drank. The
woman made some bread that was flat and
baked on the rocks. It reminded him of
the tortillas that Maria had made when
he had been at the Mims's ranch. He
wandered over and tasted some; then
dunked it into a bowl of food as he saw
the Indians do. They nodded. The
women didn't eat until all the men were
finished and wandered off. Some of the
men sat in a circle; another beat on a
hollowed-out log; many of them smoked

home-made pipes. Shamus wondered if it

was tobacco or something else in them.

He had so many questions.

When most of the Indians had

retired, Shamus went to his tent and

laid down. He slept intermittently.

When the sun peeped over a distant

mountain, Shamus rose; went to the

water and bathed his face. Not many of

the Indians were moving around; so he

went to the tent where Champ lay.

He pulled back the flap carefully. The

Medicine Man (if that is what he was)

lay asleep. Champ opened his eyes when

Shamus approached.

"It is you," he exclaimed. "I

thought I was dreaming."

"I am here," Shamus said. "Are you feeling better?"

Champ said, "Every day I get a little stronger. They have brought me back from the dead."

"Do you know who shot you?" asked Shamus.

Champ nodded. "A nasty little bugger named Dinger O'Flaherty. I found the mother lode; I mean, Shamus, I found the mother lode of all times. I was tired of my site and I wandered around, missing you, and feeling discouraged. I walked towards some rocks just outside the end of the plots and I saw an opening. When I walked inside there was gold, Shamus, real gold. It was gold from floor to ceiling. I thought I was dreaming. I thought I was seeing things, but there it was, clear as day. I was so excited and wished for you to hurry back so I could tell you I had done it."

He stopped and breathed heavily for a while.

Shamus said, "Why don't you rest for a while?"

Champ tried to nod; drool ran out the corner of his mouth.

"I hope he lives," Shamus thought and said a few prayers and crossed himself. The Medicine Man was staring at him and his eyes glittered. Shamus smiled at him but he didn't respond.

When the trappers, Mebo and Shep,
arrived, Shamus introduced himself and
told them a short version of the story.

Mebo said, "Indians kept him
alive." Shamus nodded.

"I have some questions," Shamus
said. "Would you ask the chief what
his name is?"

"Sunrise," said Shep.

"And how far are we from the gold
fields?"

"One day," said Mebo.

"Would you ask the Medicine Man
when Champ can travel?"

Both Shep and Mebo shrugged.

"What animals do you trap?" Shamus
asked.

Shep answered him.

"How do you trap and what do you do with them?" asked Shamus.

Mebo gave him a shrewd look and said, "We trade them for goods; sometimes with settlement; sometimes with fort; and sometimes with Indians."

Mebo said, "Are you gold hunter?"

"No," Shamus said, "I write stories for a newspaper."

"Oh," said Shep, "A pen man." They laughed.

Shep said shyly, "Will you write a story about me?"

"I would like to," said Shamus. "What do you want people in a big city far away to know about you?"

"I'll think on it."

The trappers talked with Chief Sunrise and some of the women bought out baskets and bowls in pretty colors. The men brought out spears and bows and arrows. The trappers haggled and traded until everyone appeared to be satisfied.

The next morning, the trappers told Shamus they were going to the fort and did he want to come with them.

"Can we take Champ with us?"

Mebo talked with the Medicine Man and Shep talked with the chief.

The traders asked Shamus could he pay the tribe for their trouble.

Shamus asked, "What would they want

that I have?"

"The Chief likes your hat and the Medicine Man wants a pencil and paper. He thinks they hold big power."

"That they do," said Shamus.

CHAPTER TWENTY

The three men laid Champ gently on piles of buffalo hides.

Shamus made a big ceremony of handing the chief his hat and the Medicine Man got a pencil and a notebook. Shamus showed the Medicine Man how to make marks in the book.

It was a long ride to Fort Friday.

Champ slept most of the time and Shamus

sang songs. The trappers liked the

music and whenever he stopped singing,

they asked for more.

     The guards of Fort Friday, heard

them coming a long way off and opened

the gates for the trappers, Shamus and

the wagon. The trappers went to the

combination saloon and trading post to

do business and have a drink; in fact,

several drinks.

     Shamus asked to see the commanding

officer and a young soldier directed

him to a door. Shamus knocked and when

he heard a gruff come in, he met with

Captain Harry Silver, a West Point

graduate, who had met Mr. Fletcher

several times. He told a subordinate to take Champ to the infirmary and have the doctor examine him. Captain Silver and Shamus sat and drank tea with soda crackers, while Shamus told the story.

"The gold field is in my jurisdiction," the Captain said. "Do you know if your friend filed his claim before this man Dinger did?"

Shamus shrugged his shoulders. "I don't know."

There was a knock on the door, and Shamus was introduced to Matthew August, the fort's physician. He was young, blonde. and had a mustache. They shook hands.

Shamus said, "How is Champ? Will

he live? Does he have bullets in him?
Is he awake?"

The doctor held up his hand at
Shamus's eagerness.

"First," he said, "I think he will
live and the bullets (three in all)
went straight through him and it
appears they missed vital organs. He
was very lucky. I gave him a sleeping
draught and bandaged him. You should
wait until tomorrow to talk to him."

"Thank you very much." said Shamus.

The doctor nodded; saluted his
Captain and left.

Shamus was taken to a barracks and
given a bed which felt better than
sleeping on the ground. He didn't

sleep very well.

CHAPTER TWENTY ONE

The trappers came to get him at dawn and took him to the Mess Hall for breakfast.

"We are leaving," Mebo said. "It has been a treat to meet you and if you ever want to learn how to trap, we would be happy to show you. We would like a story about us."

Shamus said, "I have already started to write it."

The two men waved as they rode out the gate.

Shamus went to the door with a Red Cross on it and knocked. The doctor opened the door.

The Captain was sitting next to Champ and talking quietly to him. He held some papers in his hand.

"Shamus," said Champ. "I am so happy to see you. I can't thank you enough for rescuing me."

Shamus clasped his hand and said, "What do you think Captain? Will Champ be able to claim his gold?"

The Captain handed the papers to Shamus and he saw it was a claim deed of ownership; an assay report of two gold nuggets; and the third was a telegram from Boston Mining Engineers saying they would be arriving in two weeks. Of course, the two weeks were long gone by now and Shamus wondered where they were.

The Captain stood and said, "I am
accompanying you two back to the gold
fields and helping you establish your
legal claim on the mine. We will
attempt to find the Boston Mining
Engineers, if they are still alive, and
stay on site until the mine is running.
You will need to be ready by noon."

Shamus helped Champ to his feet and
they walked slowly to the trading post
where Shamus bought Champ pants,
shirts, socks and boots. He bought two
ten-gallon hats; one for himself and
one for Champ.

"You don't have to spent money on
me," Champ said.

"You can give me a gold nugget or two in payment," Shamus smirked.

They were ready and waiting when noon came and Captain Silver called him men to attention. Sargent Muldoon brought the wagon and horse around for Shamus. They helped Champ and Shamus to the bed of the wagon and a young trooper named Sam Mason took the reins. Captain Silver and Sargent Muldoon led them out and four soldiers lined up behind.

The sun was blazing hot and Shamus was glad he had bought the wide-brimmed hats.

They made good time and when dusk began to fall, they approached the

outskirts of the gold fields. Trooper
Mason pulled up and Sargent Muldoon
came alongside the wagon. He put a
saddle blanket over the men and told
them to stay low.

The troopers pulled up in front of
the saloon and Captain Silver went
inside. He posted two troopers at the
door.

"I am looking for a man known as
Dinger," he said to the barkeep.

The man was polishing the wooden
bar and didn't stop. He said, "Nope,
not here."

"Do you know where he could be?"

"Nope."

Captain Silver saw two men trying

to slip out the front and had his troopers stopped them. The Captain went outside and pulled the two men aside.

"Where's Dinger?" he said.

"Who?" said one man.

"I can arrest you for obstruction of justice. Now, where's Dinger?"

The man pointed to a saloon across the way.

Captain Silver said, "Hold them until I return," and he walked to the saloon.

He entered and asked the man behind the bar, "I am looking for a man called Dinger."

The barkeep poured a drink and

leaned forward saying softly, "By the door, red shirt, beard, playing cards."

Captain Silver ignored the drink and walked to the card table. He pulled his gun and said, "Dinger, you are under arrest for claim jumping, attempted murder and falsifying government papers. Stand up."

Dinger looked up at him with blurry eyes.

"I ain't Dinger," he said. "My name is Jimbo." His words were slurred and his hands shook.

"Stand up," said Captain Silver. He pulled him to his feet and hauled him outside. The troopers holding the two men across the way, let them go and walked quickly to Captain Silver.

"Have him identified," Captain Silver ordered.

Shamus had climbed out of the wagon and made sure Champ was covered. When two troopers bought a man to stand in front of him, Shamus said, "This man is known as Dinger."

Captain Silver tied the man's hands and took him to the land office. When he entered he introduced himself to the agent and informed him that as an employee of the government, he was ordering him to keep Dinger locked up and tied up until business was complete.

Shamus, Captain Silver, Sargent

Muldoon, and the land agent inspected the papers that Champ had handed over. They also checked the claim that Dinger had made for the same plot and everyone was in agreement that the mine belonged to Champ.

"I haven't seen him for a long time," the agent said. "He might not even be alive."

Captain Silver gave the agent a severe look, but said nothing.

The troopers put the trussed Dinger on a horse and tied his legs together under the horse's belly. They all went to the land, now proved to be owned by Champ. The soldiers made a fire, coffee, and stew out of their supplies.

Dinger was left tied to the horse. Shamus helped Champ from the wagon and joining the Sargent and the Captain, entered the cave.

The Captain stared at the wall.

"Sweet heavens above," whispered the Sargent, "will you look at that!"

Shamus said, "there is a huge nugget farther back in the cave."

"Where is that?" Captain Silver said, pointing upwards where the stars shone through the opening.

Shamus said, "You climb to the top of the rocks and you can stare down into this place. Captain, I really need to get to the city and a telegraph office to file my articles. My boss,

Mr. Fletcher, might think I have been done in, and I hate to think who he will send to find me. He is a powerful man with lots of connections."

Captain Silver said, "Let's eat and make some plans."

After several different ideas were suggested, the Captain declared that two of his men would accompany Champ and Shamus to the city. They would stay in the hotel until he send word.

"Please check around to see if you can located the mining men sent out from the East."

CHAPTER TWENTY TWO

The Captain was leaving Sargent

Muldoon in charge and his orders were to guard the mine. No one was to enter on penalty of shoot to kill. Furthermore, the Sargent must keep Shamus and Champ guarded. He would take Dinger to the fort and incarcerate him in the stockade. He would return bringing reinforcements to the Sargent.

"I'll meet you and Champ in the city," he said to Shamus. "You men be careful; don't go anywhere without an armed escort."

Everyone had their orders and the soldiers took turns keeping guard around the site. The mining site was abuzz with all kinds of rumors; some of the men packed up and left; others left the bars early and still others made the rounds asking what was happening.

When Shamus and Champ got to the city, Shamus went to the telegraph office and picked up a handful of telegrams.

He gave the operator articles and a telegram that said he was well.

Champ sat beside him looking pale and anxious. The two troopers assigned to them stood beside them with guns over their shoulders. They wouldn't allow anyone to approach the two men, which annoyed Shamus, who would like to find out what had happened while he was gone.

He answered Mick's telegram to tell

him everything was fine, and he would write a letter very soon. Mr. Fletcher had sent numerous telegrams, each one getting more and more anxious as to what he was doing. He wrote out answers to each of Mr. Fletcher's telegram. The last one said he had found what Mr. Fletcher was looking for, but it had to be a secret until engineers arrived. He kept it vague, knowing that Mr. Fletcher would read between the lines and not let it out until it was verified.

Miss Veronica had sent her usual terse telegram that the money was in his bank account. A young lad approached him and when the soldiers

stopped him, he handed them two letters
and a pouch from the pony express
office. Mick and Mellie had both
written to him and the pouch contained
newspapers. He handed the papers to
Champ to read.

He began to write a new article
when the hotel clerk waved to him.
Shamus stood up and motioned him
forward, telling the soldiers, he
wanted him to speak.

"There were three men staying at
the hotel. They wanted to speak with
you and spent time asking everyone
where you were. I told them to go to
the mining town, but they shook their
heads. Finally, they got tired of

waiting and said if you showed up, give you this." The clerk handed over a letter.

Shamus read the letter; handed it to Champ to read; and then went to the pony express office and sent it on to Mr. Fletcher.

"Let him deal with it," he told Champ. "They shouldn't send men that are afraid of their own shadow."

Sargent Muldoon rode in with two troopers. Shamus and Champ were sure that their 'watch dogs' were happy to have some relief.

Champ, Shamus and the Sargent went to the dining hall and the Sargent said he was ordered to bring them back to the mining town. Also, they hadn't heard or seen from the mining engineers and Shamus filled him in that they had fled back east. The men laughed ruefully.

Shamus sent out his latest story; a long article regarding life in an Indian village. He gave the hotel clerk a letter that was to be delivered when one or more mining engineers arrived asking for him.

CHAPTER TWENTY THREE

Champ's mine was surrounded by

military men who kept everyone away on

penalty of being shot. Champ and

Shamus were pelted with questions, but deftly turned any answers away.

Sargent Muldoon arm wrestled with Champ and then Shamus and almost won. He was very strong. The Sargent and Shamus sang songs with the piano man and their voices blended well.

When the weekly stagecoach arrived, two men stepped down. They were dressed in heavy brown jodhpurs; white open-necked shirts and heavy boots. Champ was at his mine, picking away at smaller areas, collecting nuggets which he dropped in a pouch; but Shamus was sitting on the porch steps writing his latest article. When he spied the men, he knew they must be the mining

engineers sent by Mr. Fletcher. They
appeared to be ready for business.

When they arrived at the hotel,
Shamus stood and said, "You must be the
engineers we've been waiting to meet."

The soldier guarding Shamus stepped
forward.

Mr. Meckle and Mr. Johnson were
from Boston and were of the highest
caliber in their field. They checked
into the hotel, dropped their
belongings in their rooms and asked
Shamus to escort them to the
prospective mine. He obliged. His
armed guard followed closely.

Champ and Shamus stood outside the
mine, scuffing their boots nervously.

They were joined by Sargent Muldoon who joked with them.

"Your men are doing a fine job," Shamus told him.

Champ agreed.

Muldoon puffed up and said, "Just following orders," but they could tell he was pleased to be praised.

The engineers spent most of the day in the mine and the men got tired of waiting. They wandered into town and stopped at an eatery for a bite to eat, washed down with coffee.

"Why don't you two ever arm wrestle each other?" asked Muldoon.

Champ and Shamus glanced at each other.

Champ said, "because we are friends."

Around sunset, the engineers arrived and joined the men. They ate the 'special' and drank coffee. They shared some of their history with the men and then Mr. Meckle said softly, "we need to talk some place private."

Shamus said, "No such thing in this settlement."

Muldoon said, "The mine would be the best. My men keep everyone away."

The men walked solemnly to the mine. It was dark and the engineers lit the lamps on their hats. It didn't make it much lighter.

Everyone sat down on stones;

actually, gold; and waited.

Mr. Johnson said, "Gentlemen, this is one of the richest and most accessible strikes we have ever seen. I will wire Mr. Fletcher to arrange for all the equipment you will need to be shipped here immediately. It was a brilliant idea to arrange for the soldiers."

Champ said, "I can't believe I finally hit it big."

Shamus added, "It's a wondrous thing."

Mr. Meckle said, "we will be leaving on the next stage and when the equipment is delivered, you should hire an experienced manager to install and run it. Immediately thereafter, you should hire – oh – maybe twenty men to start. You need wagons and horses to haul the ore to the refinery. I would guess that Mr. Fletcher would like a list of all the equipment you will need. My advice, Mr. Champ, is to keep a close eye on everyone. Gold makes men greedy."

"Just plain Champ," he murmured.

Shamus said, "thank you gentlemen. You have been most efficient and I will be glad to mention your names in my next article. It will blow this place wide open."

CHAPTER TWENTY FOUR

     Shamus was right. The headline

read: EUREKA, HUGE GOLD STRIKE. Not

only were the engineers and their

company mentioned, but the United

States Army, Captain Silver and Sargent

Muldoon were highly praised.

Shamus and Champ, with the help of

Meckle and Johnson, made a long list

and sent it on to Mr. Fletcher.

"We should be in Boston in a week.

Is there anything you want us to

deliver?"

The two friends shrugged.

Shamus mailed Mick a long letter

with all the latest news. Shamus

posted a note to Mellie telling her

that his work was almost done and he

would like to stop and see her on his

way to Boston.

Shamus filled notebooks with

sketches and ideas and short comments.

Champ was the one that came up with the

idea of a hotel; after all, the ride

from the town could not be made daily and while the rough tents were okay, a hotel would be more comfortable, not to mention it would be very profitable. Shamus passed the idea on to Mr. Fletcher.

Shamus continued to send descriptive articles to Mr. Fletcher and he would print them as soon as they arrived. His newspaper was quickly becoming the number one reading material and the buzz of Boston.

Other newspapers sent reporters and Shamus was polite to them, but shared no inside information. After all, this was his story.

CHAPTER TWENTY FIVE

Champ was too busy organizing his enterprise and he surprised himself at how well it was going. As soon as a

freight wagon pulled in, it was
unloaded and the equipment set up.
Champ decided, and Shamus agreed, that
they would not take the engineers
advice to hire a manager; at least, not
yet.

A wagon loaded with tough and rough
men, wearing gun belts and displaying
lots of swagger arrived.

"We are here, Mr. Champ, to guard
your mine and your body," said their
foreman, Jack. "You can now dismiss
the Army."

Shamus and Champ were sad to see
the Captain and his men depart; but
they were particularly unhappy to lose
the company of Muldoon.

Champ said, "If you ever decide to leave the Army, you will always have a job here."

Muldoon shook hands with both men.

Every day, freight wagons arrived, loaded with supplies for the men. Carpenters were hired and a hotel was erected. The Gold Nugget Hotel had every amenity and was filled immediately. Shamus wired Mr. Fletcher, "we need another hotel; this one is over flowing."

No sooner said than done and the Hotel Champ was built and soon filled.

CHAPTER TWENTY SIX

There were other entrepreneurs that came to the settlement and built dining facilities and supply stores. One day

a China man arrive with his family and

opened a laundry. He was busy and

getting rich. An enterprising woman

arrived and opened a bath. She hired

attractive attendants and men flocked

to wash up at the end of the day.

Shamus reported everything.

The day came when he received a

telegram from Mr. Fletcher.

It read, "I think it's time for you

to come home."

Shamus and Champ got rousing drunk

and cried on each other's shoulders all

night long. As soon as Shamus

recovered sufficiently, he hitched a

ride on a freight wagon.

Champ gave Shamus two large gold nuggets as going away gifts. One was for him and the other for Mr. Fletcher.

"I'll be back some day," Shamus said sadly.

CHAPTER TWENTY SEVEN

When Shamus arrived at the train depot, he bought his ticket for the first lap of his journey. His first stop was at the town near Mellie, and he would find a way to her ranch somehow.

The town was small; didn't even have a telegraph office. Shamus got down from the train and he was glad to

stretch his legs. One of the first
sights he saw, was Mellie and her
foreman coming out of the supply store.

"Mellie, Mellie," he called as she
climbed into the loaded wagon.

The cowhand pulled the wagon around
to him and Mellie hopped down.

"Well, it's about time you
arrived," she said. "I thought you
would never get here."

Shamus talked the entire time they
traveled to the ranch. His stories
were humorous and entertaining and
Mellic hung on his every word.

"Where is Bradford?" Shamus asked
when they pulled up to the main house
and he wasn't on the porch.

Mellie looked sad. "He passed a few months back."

"Oh no," said Shamus. "That's sad."

"Well," Mellie said stiffly, "it was a relief really.   It was hard to take care of him and he was getting meaner every day. I would rather remember the happy times. He was a fine Pa before his accident."

Shamus greeted Maria, "I'm back for your tortillas."

She smiled at him.

Mellie and Shamus walked around the ranch. "I have to teach you how to ride," she said. "This walking is not for me."

They spent all their waking hours together. It was a sad day when Shamus announced he was leaving the next day.

The bunkhouse cook prepared a fine feast and Shamus sang accompanied by the guitar-playing cowboy.

Mellie said, "Shamus, I want to discuss some business with you." They sat on the porch drinking coffee, laced with whiskey.

She thought carefully and then said, "It is hard work to keep a ranch this size running smoothly. I have come to the conclusion that I need a partner." She stopped talking. When she started again, it was obvious that she had put a lot of thought into it.

"When you were here before, you said that your cousin Mick and his family should be raising their family in a place such as this."

At first Shamus thought she was asking him to be a partner, but then she mentioned Mick and Mary. He was disappointed. He had thought she was going to propose that he become her partner.

"Do you want to be a reporter forever?" she asked.

Shamus shook his head.

"I think I have had enough this last year to last a lifetime. Maybe I'll write a book."

Mellie said, "Or help me run a

ranch. There would be a lot to learn and I expect you and Mick to work hard. I don't want any slackers around."

Shamus was thrilled. "I'll have to discuss it with Mick and Mary, of course, but I am sure I can convince them they should move west. I can be very persuasivc." He grinned.

"I bet you can," Mellie grinned back. She appeared to be waiting for him to say more, but Shamus was a thinking man and not a;ways quick on decisions.

CHAPTER TWENTY-EIGHT

The next morning, Mellie and a cowhand drove Shamus to the station. They had breakfast at a cafe and then went to the depot to await the train. It wasn't long in coming.

Shamus turned to Mellie and gathered her in his arms and planted a big, passionate kiss on her upturned face. She gasped and waved good-bye from the platform as the train puffed away.

"Oh, yes," she said, "You can be very persuasive."

Mr. Fletcher, to the shock of the entire newsroom, grabbed Shamus and hugged him, swinging him around and clapping him on the shoulder.

"Oh, my boy, I'm am so happy to see you."

"I'm happy to be back," Shamus said. "I haven't even been home yet."

"Take the rest of the day off," beamed Mr. Fletcher. "Come breakfast with me tomorrow morning. I know we have hours of talking to do."

Shamus thought if he only knew what's coming.

When he got to the third-floor walk-up, the door was locked so he banged loudly.

Mary opened the door a slit and then threw it wide.

"Shamus, Shamus," she cried and

hugged his neck. "Mick, Mick, get your lazy fanny out here; the prodigal son has returned."

Mick came from the kitchen with pants and an undershirt on. His feet were bare and his eyes were blood shot and blurry. Shamus was shocked at his appearance.

Mick smiled and grabbed Shamus, dancing around.

"Well, old sod, you finally brought yourself back. I'm so glad to see you. Come and sit down and eat and drink and tell us all your stories. I read the newspapers but I want to know the untold stories. All the gory details."

They talked all day until Mary had

to collect the twins and Shannon from

school. Rohan and Rodney were thrilled

to see their uncle and asked a million

questions, not even waiting for the

answers.

Shamus said, "A delivery van should

be bringing my belongings here today."

Mick laughed, "Too big and famous

to carry your own valises."

Shamus looked around, noticing that

the cupboards were bare and that the

good smells that usually poured from

Mary's kitchen were missing.

Shamus took a large sum of money

from his pocket and said, "Mary, go buy

some special things for my coming home

party. I'm longing for your fabulous

cooking."

After Mary had departed, taking the twins with her to carry things, Shamus turned to Mick.

"Still out of work, hey?"

Mick nodded. "I went back and then the owners went back on their agreement with the Union, so I'm out again. I try to pick up spare jobs, but so does every other longshoreman." He shrugged. "Thanks to you we have been okay." He poked Shamus on the arm.

"Now that the lady copper is gone, let's have a drink. She guards this bottle with her life." Shamus and Mick drank a short glass and when Mick went to pour another, Shamus stopped him.

"I have a proposition for you.
Don't say no until you have heard me
out to the end." He began by
describing the west; the wide open
spaces; the huge ranch; and then told
Mick that a lady named Mellie owned it.

"Aha," said Mick, "I should have
guessed a lovely lady was behind this."

"Partly," said Shamus, "but I was
already playing the idea around in my
head. I want to move west, but I just
can't leave you and your family behind.
Mellie has offered us a partnership in
the ranch. After having been away, the
city seems more crowded and smelly than
ever. It's not good for the wee ones
to be packed in here. I keep

remembering the times we had in County Cork, running through the fields, working the potatoes, and feeling the sweat of honest labor."

Mary arrived. The boys were loaded down and so was Mary. She gave Shamus the change and said, "You boy's go down to the pub. Now, mind you, don't get drunk, just stay long enough for me to cook a feast and invite everyone to a party."

Shamus and Mick did as directed. Shamus remarked at how many people liked Mick and greeted both men with enthusiasm and joy.

The party lasted most of the night and when Shamus stumbled around getting dressed to go meet Mr. Fletcher, he saw his family stretched out in various positions. He left money on the table and put the sugar jar on top of it.

Mr. Fletcher and Shamus spent the morning talking and reveling in Champ's good fortune, which was their good fortune as well. Shamus presented the large gold nugget, Champ had sent him. He was pleased.

"Tonight," said Mr. Fletcher, "you are invited to a Board meeting at seven o'clock. The members want to show their appreciation for your out-standing work I suggest you spend the rest of the week, preparing to come in on Monday. Just because you are famous, does not mean you can rest on your laurels."

Shamus arrived home to find Mick and Mary in a serious discussion. Shamus thought that Mary had been weeping. The kitchen had delicious smells which made Shamus glad. A baby was crying in the bedroom, so Mary went to feed him.

"What do you think?" asked Shamus. "I need to tell Mr. Fletcher right away if I am leaving, but I'm not leaving without you. I have missed you too much for too long and I'm not doing it again."

Mick shrugged. "She's a hard sell, she is. Doesn't want to leave her friends; school for the boys; or her precious possessions she brought from the Old Country."

"Let's just go and visit." Shamus said. "We don't have to make any decisions until you both have seen the country and looked around."

Mick looked shocked. "Do you know how much it will cost for us all to travel there and back?"

"I believe I do," said Shamus.

CHAPTER TWENTY NINE

Shamus dressed his best and left for the Board meeting. He was well-received and answered numerous questions about the west and the value of the gold and how long it would be before it would run out.. They seemed pleased with his answers and shook hands with him before he left.

"See you on Monday," said Mr.

Fletcher.

When Shamus got home, Mary was in bed, the children were asleep and Mick was out. He went to bed and said his prayers as he had all his life.

"It's in your hands," he whispered to God in heaven.

THE END